lchemist❖alchemy❖algebra❖align❖allegory❖alopecia❖amazement❖amber❖amethyst❖amu

rmadillo❖armlet❖armour❖army❖arrow❖asparagus❖astray❖astrolabe❖astronomer❖astrono

ird❖bison❖bite❖black❖blue❖blush❖blushing❖boat❖bob❖bold❖bolt❖bone❖book❖bounce❖bounced❖bow❖boy❖brass

ng❖camel❖camlet❖camouflage❖canary❖candelabra❖candle❖candlestick❖canister❖canopy❖canteen❖cape❖carrying

arts❖check❖cheese❖chef❖chequered❖chest❖chestnut❖chimpanzee❖chipmunk❖chirp❖choice❖chortle❖chuckle❖circle

r❖coupe❖couple❖crab❖crack❖crazy❖crescent❖crest❖crimson❖crocodile❖cross❖crossbow❖crown❖crystal❖crystal ball

gn❖device❖diagonal❖diagram❖dial❖diamond❖diaphanous❖dinner❖dinosaur❖dish❖dismay❖dividers❖dodo❖dome

ink❖drop❖drum❖drumstick❖duck❖dupe❖eagle❖ear❖earring❖earth❖east❖eat❖eccentric❖eclipse❖edge❖egg❖eggcup

ounter❖end❖ensign❖enterprise❖envelope❖epaulet❖equator❖equinox❖err❖escape❖espadrilles❖exasperated❖exotic

on❖falling❖fans❖fast❖fastening❖fat❖fawning❖feather❖feet❖fellow❖felt❖fence❖fez❖fin❖find❖finger❖fingernail❖fire

ags❖flagstone❖flame❖flat❖fletching❖flight❖flights❖floating❖flocking❖florid❖flower❖fluffy❖flute❖fluttering❖flying

l❖fox❖fragile❖fragment❖frayed❖freckles❖free❖friend❖frill❖fringe❖frog❖frown❖full❖fulvous❖fur❖fusilier❖gabble

tle❖geography❖gesture❖giant❖gift❖gigantic❖girdle❖girl❖girth❖give❖glance❖glaucous❖glider❖globe❖glove❖glum

❖grass❖grasshopper❖grate❖green❖grey❖grill❖grim❖grimace❖grip❖grooves❖ground❖guide❖guineapig❖gyroscope

r❖hearts❖heavy❖helmet❖helping❖hen❖henna❖heraldry❖heron❖hexagon❖hiding❖hieroglyphics❖hiking❖hill❖hinge

rse❖horseshoe❖hourglass❖ibex❖ibis❖iceberg❖icon❖ideograph❖igloo❖iguana❖illustration❖image❖imago❖immure

al❖ink❖innocent❖inscription❖insect❖inset❖inside❖intent❖intersect❖intricate❖intrigue❖involute❖iris❖irons❖irregular

y❖journey❖joust❖joyful❖jug❖juggle❖jute❖kaleidoscope❖kangaroo❖kayak❖keel❖keep❖keg❖kern❖kettle❖kettledrum

wi❖knapsack❖knave❖knee❖knight❖knit❖knob❖knot❖knuckle❖koala❖koan❖kudos❖label❖labour❖labyrinth❖lace

ance❖lantern❖lap❖lapel❖lappet❖large❖lariat❖larrikin❖lashings❖lasso❖last❖latch❖latitude❖lattice❖laugh❖lavender

ege❖light❖lighthouse❖lightning❖lilac❖lime❖limn❖line❖linear❖link❖linkwork❖lion❖lip❖list❖little❖lively❖lizard❖load

❖mace❖magenta❖magnet❖magnify❖magnifying glass❖magpie❖mail❖male❖mallet❖mammals❖mammoth❖mandarin

tape❖medal❖medley of maps❖meeting❖melon❖memorable❖mend❖merciful❖message❖message-in-a-bottle❖messy

❖moving❖music❖nab❖nail❖Napoleon Mouse❖Napoleonic❖narwhal❖nascent❖naughty❖near❖nebulous❖needle❖nest

otes❖nought❖noughts and crosses❖number❖nurse❖nurture❖oar❖oarsman❖oasis❖obelisk❖obfuscation❖object❖objects

id❖octagon❖octant❖octoped❖octopus❖odd❖offer❖offsider❖off-white❖ogle❖ogling❖oh❖old❖old-world❖olive❖one

❖outwit❖oval❖overbearing❖overcome❖ovoid❖owl❖pace❖pack❖paddle❖padlock❖pail❖paint❖paintbrush❖pair❖paisley

arrot❖part❖passenger❖passing❖patch❖patchwork❖paunch❖paw❖pawn❖pearls❖peculiar❖peep❖peer❖peg leg❖pelage

ersuade❖pettitoes❖pewter❖pi❖pick❖pickaxe❖pied❖pier❖pig❖piglet❖pigtail❖pillars❖pineapples❖pinion❖pink❖pinnacle

e❖plummet❖plumose❖plunder❖plunger❖pocket❖point❖poke❖pole❖polka-dots❖porky❖port❖pose❖pot❖precarious

urple❖purposeful❖push❖quad❖quadrangle❖quadrant❖quadrate❖quadrilateral❖quadruped❖quadruplet❖quail❖quaint

uestion mark❖queue❖quibble❖quiet❖quiff❖quill❖quilt❖quilted map❖quintain❖quintuplet❖quiver❖quizzical❖quoits

❖raiment❖rain❖rainbow❖rainproof❖rake❖ram❖ramification❖rampart❖rapids❖rapt❖rascal❖rash❖rasp❖ratine❖ratline

❖relief motif❖remarkable❖repair❖repine❖resting❖retard❖reverberate❖rhinoceros❖rhombus❖riant❖ribbon❖ricochet

ow❖rowing❖royal blue❖rubiginous❖ruby❖rucksack❖rudder❖ruin❖ruminant❖rump❖rung❖running❖rush❖rushes❖russet

e❖sand❖sandal❖sapphire❖sash❖saucepan❖save❖saw❖sawfish❖scabbard❖scallywag❖scan❖scarf❖scarlet❖scatterbrain

❖seagull❖seal❖seaman❖search❖seat❖see❖seeking❖selachion❖semaphore❖semicircle❖sentient❖serpent❖set of sails

sinister❖sinking sailor❖sinking ship❖sisal❖sitting❖six❖skating❖skunk❖sky❖sleeve❖slipping❖slow❖sly❖smell❖smile

pray❖squall❖squares❖staircase❖stalwart❖stand❖stars❖stash❖staves❖steadfast❖steeve❖stench❖stern❖stink❖stitches

nbol❖tablecloth❖tache❖taciturn❖tail❖talisman❖talons❖tame❖tan❖tankard❖target❖tartan❖task❖tassel❖taunt❖taut❖team

nb❖tick❖tied❖tiger❖tight❖tigress❖tin❖tip❖toad❖toadstool❖toby jug❖toe❖toecap❖toggle❖tongue❖toot❖torch❖torn

❖tricky❖trumpet❖trumpeting❖tubular❖tulip❖tunic❖turkey❖turquoise❖twelve❖twenty❖twined❖twins❖twisted❖two

ants❖undertaking❖underwear❖undone❖undulating❖uneven❖unfastened❖unfortunate❖unhappy❖unhook❖unicorn

❖varied❖vase❖vegetable❖veil❖vent❖vermilion❖vertex❖vertical❖vertices❖vertigo❖vessel❖vest❖vested❖veteran

y❖vixen❖volant❖volcano❖volitant❖volute❖voyage❖vulture❖wadding❖waders❖waist❖waistband❖waistcoat

arted❖warp❖watch❖watching❖water❖waterborne❖waterfall❖watering can❖waterworks❖wave❖waver❖way

t❖weighty❖well❖well-balanced❖wellbeing❖well-built❖wending❖west❖westering❖westwards❖wet❖whale

icker basket❖wickerwork❖wide❖wilful❖will❖willing❖willy-nilly❖wily❖wind❖windmill❖winsome❖wise

den❖woof❖words❖working❖worm❖worthwhile❖worthy❖wound❖woven❖wrinkles❖wrist❖writing❖xeric

in❖zestful❖zig-zag❖zingaro❖zinnia❖zippy❖zircon❖zodiac❖and many many more words for you to find

We're going on a quest!
Come, join the fun…

Welcome to our world of words and images which we offer to you, the reader ~ the young and the young at heart.

We spent many hours poring over a dictionary and found hundreds of different kinds of words to include in this book ~ and then enjoyed hiding them in the illustrations. Look out for the hidden letter on each page ~ some will be easy to find, but others will be difficult.

There are hundreds of words and ideas illustrated throughout the book. There's loads of fun to be had making up stories and crazy poems using them all. Look for the horse who has his own special story ~ it starts on "H" and ends on the "L" page. And there's the gorilla gazing glumly on the globe because the fox has filched a fragment of his map! Each page is linked to the next and the story is continuous. It is our journey, our quest.

Let the characters and their stories capture your imagination as they captured ours!

Come, play with this book. It is a gift of language and we ask you to join the fun and to aim your arrow high.

Bruce Whatley and Rosie Smith

Whatley's QUEST

WRITTEN BY

Bruce Whatley & Rosie Smith

ILLUSTRATED BY

Bruce Whatley

Angus&Robertson
An imprint of HarperCollinsPublishers

For Mum whose love and perseverance gave me
the gift of my right arm. And for Dad ~a true craftsman.
Bruce

For Mum with love and in loving memory of Dad.
Rosie

For our children, Ben and Ellyn.
Thank you for your inspiration and patience.
May your aim be true.
Love from Mum and Dad

An Angus & Robertson Publication

Angus&Robertson, an imprint of
HarperCollins*Publishers*
25 Ryde Road, Pymble, Sydney, NSW 2073, Australia
31 View Road, Glenfield, Auckland 10, New Zealand

First published in Australia in 1994
Reprinted in 1994

Copyright © Farmhouse Illustration Company Pty Limited, 1994

National Library of Australia
Cataloguing-in-Publication data:

Whatley, Bruce.
    Whatley's quest.
    ISBN 0 207 18491 7.
    1. Alphabet – Juvenile literature. I. Smith, Rosie, 1956-
    II. Title.
421.1

Printed in Hong Kong
7 6 5 4 3 2
97 96 95 94

Archer, draw back your bow
for you will direct our journey.

Our Quest~
the pursuit of knowledge
and the gathering of wisdom.

Archer, aim your arrow high,
and may your aim be true.

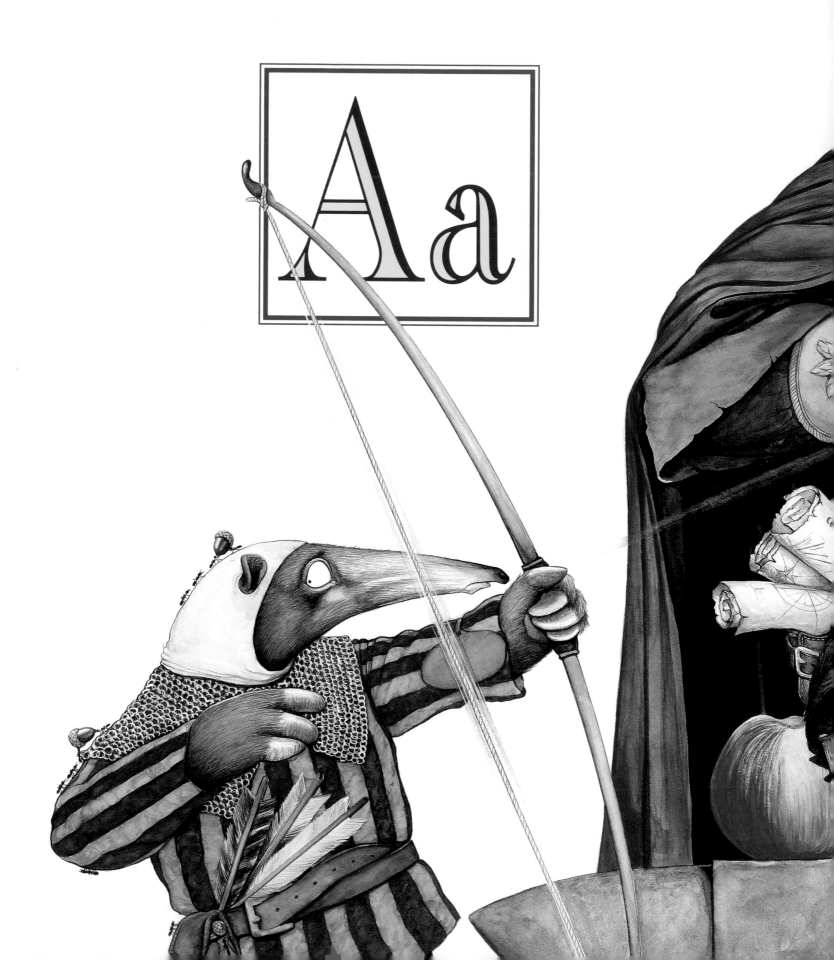

Bb

Oo

Pp

Rr

Uu
Vv

Now it is your Quest…
Always aim your arrow high,
and may your aim be true.

agtkfsBnuiopKnowledgerbcKeyxehcMhiad

igktreasurejsaDiscoveryHzyujomJoyasDGhi

oewiehtgrlnjourneyLbxcuqfawpvsdrftkjiufloenbar

xaroNwrpsuveaimbervtrueqotbizyujmaxmeft

ucarfgtvlnwisdomtLbxcuqfawpvsdrftkjiufloenbvfgty

hyselBOwrnevsypoglexvtiArrowghbwtnkcsaftg

qrvluawisdomwHjntriumphiBEOthujdbtoivl

imaRfgtvlndiscoveryxcuqfawpjoyrftkjiufloenbvfg

fipnadzvxoKqehtgrlnjourneyLbxcuqfawpl

wyRabuCasnevpevabhlaxybEjfpnbvdntgab

oseloAiCnbuieyhlervtiAlbeavwtocsziesabdvud

dRfbaxnASRntruewyhlervtiKnowledgencugs

abacus❖ability❖able❖above❖accident❖accountant❖accurate❖achieve❖acorn❖action❖add❖adversary❖advise❖aim❖al
animal❖annoying❖answer❖ant❖antagonist❖anteater❖antique❖ants❖anvil❖anxious❖apple❖appliqué❖arc❖archer❖arder
❖axe❖back❖bag❖ball❖banana❖banner❖baseball❖baseball glove❖basket❖bat❖beak❖bear❖behind❖bell❖belt❖beret❖bi
bronze❖brooding❖brown❖brown bear❖buffalo❖bull❖bullock❖bunting❖burly❖butterfly❖button❖buttonhole❖cage❖c
carved❖castellations❖castle❖caterpillar❖Celtic cross❖chain❖chair❖challenge❖chameleon❖champion❖character❖chart
clairvoyant❖claw❖cloak❖cloudy❖cob❖cobweb❖collar❖column❖comet❖compass❖cone❖consult❖cook❖cord❖core❖co
❖curls❖curly❖cushion❖dagger❖dais❖dame❖damsel❖danger❖day❖dazed❖dead❖decoy❖deduce❖deer❖defiant❖dema
dome-headed❖dominoes❖donkey❖dot❖doubtful❖down❖dozen❖dragon❖drake❖drape❖drawing❖dreadful❖dreaming
eggshell❖Egyptian❖eight❖elaborate❖elbow❖elegant❖elephant❖eleven❖elf❖embarrass❖emblem❖emerald❖empty❖e
expedition❖exploration❖expression❖eye❖eyeball❖eyeballing❖eyeful❖eyesight❖fable❖fabric❖face❖facial❖faggot❖fait
fish❖fishing basket❖fishing line❖fishing rod❖fist❖five❖five o'clock shadow❖fixated❖flag❖flag bearer❖flageolet❖fla
folded❖folds❖follow❖foot❖footslogger❖force❖forearm❖forefinger❖forehead❖foresight❖fork❖forward❖foul deed❖f
gaggle❖gamekeeper❖gander❖gargantuan❖garment❖garnet❖garnish❖gash❖gate❖gauntlet❖gawking❖gazing❖geese❖g
goanna❖goat❖go-between❖goblet❖goggles❖going❖gold❖golden egg❖goldfish❖gong❖goose❖gorilla❖gosh❖granny
hair❖halter❖hamster❖hand❖handkerchief❖handle❖hank❖happy❖harangue❖hare❖harp❖hat❖haversack❖hawking❖hav
hippopotamus❖hive❖hoe❖hoist❖holding❖hole❖holler❖honeycomb❖honk❖hood❖hoof❖hook❖hoop❖hop❖horn❖horr
impact❖imperfect❖impinge❖implement❖impossible❖imprison❖in❖Indian❖indigo❖individual❖inertia❖ingenious❖ing
❖island❖italic❖ivy❖jack❖jacket❖jade❖jam-packed❖jape❖japer❖jar❖jaw❖jester❖jewel❖jewellery❖jigsaw❖jocose❖jocu
key❖keyhole❖keyring❖keystone❖khaki❖kick❖kid❖kilt❖kiltie❖kind❖kindling❖king❖kingfisher❖kink❖kirtle❖kith
lacerated❖laces❖lacing❖lackadaisical❖lacuna❖lad❖ladder❖laden❖ladle❖lady❖ladybird❖lag❖lamb❖lambent❖lament
laying❖leaf❖lean❖leaping❖learn❖leather❖ledge❖left❖leg❖leggings❖lemon❖length❖lens❖leopard❖letter❖lettering❖lev
❖loaded❖lobster❖lock❖locket❖locks❖locus❖lolling❖long❖longitude❖look❖loop❖lounging❖love❖lucky❖lump❖lurch
mango❖manhandle❖map❖maple leaf❖marble❖maroon❖mascot❖massif❖mast❖mastodon❖mauve❖maze❖measure❖me
metal❖metric❖milestone❖military❖mitten❖mole❖moleskins❖monocle❖moon❖moose❖motif❖mound❖mountain❖mous
net❖nightdress❖nightgown❖nightingale❖nine❖ninety❖noble❖nook❖noose❖north❖nose❖nostril❖notation❖notches❖note
obligation❖oblique❖oblong❖obnoxious❖observe❖obstacle❖obstruct❖obverse❖obvious❖occupant❖occurrence❖ochr
onions❖oops❖open-mouthed❖opposition❖opt❖orange❖orang-utan❖orb❖ordeal❖ordinary❖orifice❖origami❖orle❖ornery
❖paletot❖pallor❖palm❖palm frond❖pan❖panda❖panel❖panic❖pantograph❖pants❖paper❖parallel❖parcel❖parchment❖p
pelican❖penalty❖pendant❖penguin❖penna❖pennant❖pennon❖perched❖peregrination❖peril❖periphery❖perplexed❖pers
❖piping❖pirate❖piscivorous pelican❖pitchfork❖plank❖pleat❖plight❖plug❖plumage❖plumate❖plumb❖plumb-bob❖p
preparation❖presiding❖prickly❖proboscis❖prod❖protest❖prow❖pull❖pumpkin❖punish❖punishment❖pupil❖puppet❖p
quality❖qualms❖quandary❖quarrel❖quarry❖quarter❖quartet❖quartz❖quaver❖quay❖queen❖quell❖querulous❖query
quokka❖quotation marks❖quotes❖rabbit❖rabble-rouser❖raccoon❖race❖racketeer❖radiating❖raft❖rag❖ragged❖ragge
rattle❖ray❖reaction❖reading❖realm❖rear❖rebus❖reckless❖rectangle❖red❖red ribbon❖reed❖reef knot❖regal❖relic❖re
ridiculous❖rigging❖right❖ring❖risible❖rising sun❖rivage❖river❖rivets❖rock❖rocking❖rodent❖rogue❖rope❖rose❖round
❖rust❖sable❖sack❖sad❖saddle❖sadsack❖safe❖safeguard❖sagging❖sagittal❖sail❖sailor❖salient❖sallet❖sally forth❖salti
scheming❖science❖scissors❖scoop❖screen❖screw❖screwdriver❖scroll❖scrutiny❖scrying❖scutcheon❖sea❖seaborne❖s
seven❖sextant❖shark❖sharp❖shells❖shelter❖shield❖ship❖shirt❖shoe❖shoulder❖shovel❖shroud❖sideburns❖sight❖signa
snake❖snout❖snow❖snow leopard❖snowcloud❖sock❖sortie❖south❖spade❖spanner❖spider❖spindrift❖spiral❖splash
stitching❖store❖stouthearted❖stow❖straps❖stubble❖stud❖sun❖surf❖surfing❖survey❖swan❖swashbuckling❖swinging❖sw
❖teapot❖tear❖teasing❖telescope❖ten❖tethered❖texture❖thimble❖thistle❖thorn❖thorny❖threat❖three❖thrilling❖throu
torque❖tortoise❖toucan❖tourists❖tow❖toward❖towards❖tower❖towrope❖trail❖transit❖travellers❖travelling❖treasure
umbrage❖umbrella❖unbearable❖unbolt❖unbuttoned❖unceremonious❖uncork❖uncovered❖under❖underarm❖underline
uniform❖united❖unlock❖unlucky❖unruffled❖up❖uphold❖uplift❖upon❖upset❖upside-down❖upstream❖upturn❖valian
vex❖viaduct❖vicinage❖vicinity❖Viking❖vim❖vimen❖vincible❖vine❖viola❖violate❖violence❖violet❖violin❖virtuou
waistline❖waiting❖wale❖walk❖walking❖walkway❖wall-eyed❖walnut❖walrus❖wandering❖wanderlust❖want❖ward
wayfarer❖wayfaring❖wayward❖wayworn❖wealth❖wear and tear❖wearing❖weary❖weasel❖weathered❖web❖wee❖we
wharf❖Whatley❖wheat❖wheel❖wheelbarrow❖whet❖whim❖whim-wham❖whimsical❖whiskers❖white❖wholehearted
wishbone❖wisp❖wizard❖woebegone❖wolf❖wombat❖wonder❖wonderment❖wonderstruck❖wondrous❖wood❖woodbo
x-ray fish❖xylophone❖yabber❖yacht❖yak❖yap❖yapok❖yarn❖yellow❖yes❖yoke❖youthful❖zany❖zealous❖zebra❖zenith